Evan Jacobs

SADDLEBACK
EDUCATIONAL PUBLISHING

red rhino books®

With more titles on the way . . .

SADDLEBACK
EDUCATIONAL PUBLISHING
www.sdlback.com

ISBN: 978-1-63889-046-1
eBook: 978-1-64598-861-8

Printed in Malaysia

26 25 24 23 22   1 2 3 4 5

Andrew

Age: 11 years and 362 days

Known For: Epic parties and pranks

Biggest Secret: Used to be uncool

Career Goal: Host his own prank show

Best Quality: Life of the party

Zach

Age: 11.5

Known For: Uncool clothes

Biggest Secret: Holds the highest score ever in *Clan Castles*

Career Goal: Engineer

Best Quality: Forgives others

1

THE TEXT

"OMG!" Andrew Lu shouted. "My party is going to be awesome!"

It was lunchtime. Andrew sat at a long green table. His best friends, Scott Vargas and Derek Williams, sat with him. The boys were in seventh grade at Knight Middle School.

Scott smiled. "If it's anything like the last one, it'll be epic."

We had an inflatable obstacle course AND a magician!

"Are you really getting a waterslide?" Derek asked.

"Yep." Andrew grinned. "My dad ordered it last weekend. We got the biggest one. This will be the best 12th birthday ever!"

It's over 40 feet tall!

Behold, the Splash Slide 9000!

Andrew was the coolest guy in their grade. He threw the best parties. Everyone wanted to be invited.

He also loved jokes. Pranking people was Andrew's favorite way to have fun. The best part was that he rarely got in trouble.

Once, he put fake spiders in a teacher's desk drawer. She just laughed.

In sixth grade, Andrew ran for class president. He walked around school shaking people's hands. But there was a surprise. His hand had a buzzer. When kids shook hands with him, they got shocked.

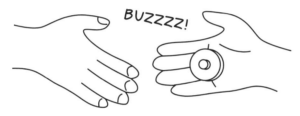

BUZZZZ!

Andrew still won. Most kids thought his pranks were funny. They never knew what he would do next.

"There will be a ton of video games," Andrew said. "Some are old. But most are new. I've got all the consoles."

"What about food?" Derek asked. He was always hungry.

"There'll be so much food. My mom hired a caterer."

"Can we have all the soda we want?" Scott asked.

"Of course," Andrew said confidently.

"What about candy?" Derek asked.

Andrew rolled his eyes. "Um, yeah! Anything you can think of, we'll have it."

all the candy you can eat

His family was rich. They lived in the biggest house in town. Andrew usually got anything he wanted.

Scott sounded excited. "I can't wait to ride that waterslide. Is it really as big as your backyard?"

Andrew's house had a huge yard. There was a pool at one end. The waterslide would be set up at the other end. Its slide was so long that it ended at the pool.

Andrew laughed. "Would I lie?" Then he remembered something. "There will be movies too."

"Really?" Derek asked.

"Yeah. My dad is having a huge screen set up. We can watch while we slide."

Just then, Zach Bottoms walked by. Zach usually wore button-down shirts. He had thick glasses. His hair was always a mess. Some kids called him a nerd.

5

Zach was nothing like Andrew and his friends. They always looked cool. Their closets were full of nice T-shirts and hoodies. None of them wore button-down shirts.

Cool   Cool   Uncool

Derek laughed. "OMG. You should invite Zach."

Scott smirked. "Yeah. Then when he accepts, tell him you were kidding. Say there's no way he can come to your party!"

"He'll be so bummed," Derek said. "Can you imagine?"

Andrew laughed. "Okay." Then he looked down. He loved pranks. Still, this felt mean.

Scott and Derek stared at him.

"Well? Are you going to do it?" Scott asked.

Andrew swallowed. He pulled out his phone. Then he quickly typed a text.

"Hey, Zach. Long time, no talk! My birthday party is on Friday. Want to come?"

He showed the text to Scott and Derek. They laughed.

Then Andrew hit send.

It's just a prank... right?

2

ZACH FROM THE PAST

"Wait." Scott looked confused. "Why do you have Zach's number?"

Andrew's face turned bright red. He and Zach had been best friends in fifth grade. They used to hang out all the time. The boys loved video games.

Zach's dad worked for GLive. That was a game company. They made *Clan Castles*. It had been Andrew and Zach's favorite game.

But things had changed. Andrew started noticing how uncool Zach was. He dressed like a nerd. That had made Andrew worry. *Does being Zach's friend make me look bad?*

nerdy shirt

What's with all the pockets?

So uncool!

Then Andrew thought Zach had lied to him. Zach told him he was going to get a download code. It was for a new *Clan Castles* game. The game had not been released yet. Only Andrew would have it. This would be Zach's birthday gift to him.

But the code never came. Andrew and Zach got in a big fight.

"You're a liar," Andrew had said. "And a nerd! We can't be friends anymore."

Andrew stopped inviting Zach over. He hung out with Scott and Derek instead. But they weren't into video games. They cared more about clothes and music. It wasn't as much fun as hanging out with Zach. But Scott and Derek were cool. This made Andrew feel cool too.

This is what I'm into now.

Later, Zach told Andrew something. He had tried to get the code. But GLive had made a new company rule. They did not want people to copy their games. It broke the law. That meant no more early download codes. Zach hadn't lied after all.

That was almost two years ago. The boys had not spoken since then.

Sometimes Andrew missed Zach. But he didn't want to reach out to him. Besides, he liked being cool.

BEING COOL > HAVING FUN

Andrew still had not answered Scott's question.

"Earth to Andrew," Derek said. "Why do you have Zach's number?"

Andrew shrugged. "I don't know. He lives near me. My mom knows his mom. She probably put it in my phone. Maybe it was in case I needed a ride home."

Just then, the bell rang. Everyone headed to class.

Shannon Evers walked past them. Kids thought she was the prettiest girl at school. Andrew had a crush on her.

Shannon Evers

"Hey, Andrew!" Shannon smiled. "I can't wait for your big party!" She waved and kept walking.

"OMG!" Derek said. "Shannon's coming?"

"Of course," Andrew said. He tried to

stay cool. But he was excited. His party was going to be awesome.

Scott and Derek had P.E. class next. They headed to the gym.

Andrew kept walking to English class. On the way, his phone buzzed. He took it out of his pocket.

A text flashed on the screen. It was from Zach.

"Birthday party? I'm in!" Zach wrote. "It'll be just like the old days!"

3

TEXT GONE WRONG

The last bell rang. Andrew met up with Scott and Derek. They always walked home together after school.

Andrew told them about the text. "Can you believe it?" he asked. "Zach thinks he's really invited."

Derek laughed. "Too funny."

"But wait," Scott said. "What if he tells

people? Then everyone will think you invited a nerd. No one will want to come."

What no one wants at a party:

clowns healthy food nerds

Andrew stopped walking. "Really? You think so? They won't come because of Zach?"

Derek nodded. "Totally. They'll think it's not cool. Text him back. Now! Tell him he can't come."

Andrew texted. "Hey. You're not invited to my party. Sorry." Then he sent the text.

"There," Andrew said. "Done." He smiled at Scott and Derek. "Problem solved."

Derek sighed. "That was a close call."

"Too close," Scott added.

The three of them laughed.

Secretly, Andrew felt bad. Zach was a good guy. But this party meant a lot to Andrew. It had to be the best ever. He couldn't risk Zach showing up.

"Any new jokes planned for Friday?" Scott asked Andrew. "You are the master."

Andrew grinned. "I've got some ideas."

"Tell us!" Derek demanded.

"Yeah," Scott said. "We're your best friends."

"How does putting dry ice in the pool sound?" Andrew asked.

pool   dry ice   epic fog!

Scott's eyes widened. "No way."

Derek gasped. "OMG!"

"Right?" Andrew grinned. "Can you imagine? People would freak out. I wonder where I can get some."

"Uh, bro," Scott said. "You've got bigger problems."

Andrew looked at his friends. They were staring at their phones.

"Wow." Derek shook his head. "This is bad."

"What?" Andrew asked.

Scott turned his phone around.

Andrew squinted at it. There was his last text to Zach. "Wait. How did you get that? I only sent it to Zach."

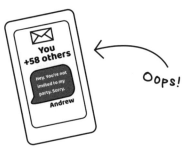

Oops!

Hey. You're not invited to my party. Sorry.

Andrew

You +58 others

18

"No, dude," Derek said. "I got it too."

"How?" Andrew looked at his phone. His face fell. "Oh no. I sent it to—"

"Everyone." Derek finished Andrew's sentence.

"It's okay. I can send another text." Andrew tried to stay calm. "I'll tell them I was just kidding."

Scott shook his head. "People are already talking. It's all over MidZone."

MidZone was a social media site. It was for middle schoolers. They all shared things about their lives. Gossip was big on the site too.

"Yikes." Derek made a face.

Scott scrolled through the posts. "Everyone is confused. Some people are mad."

Andrew went to the site too. "OMG!"

This is a mess, he thought. *I never should have sent that text. It wasn't even my idea. How can I save my party?*

4

WEB OF CONFUSION

Andrew was getting a lot of texts. The MidZone posts didn't stop either. Everyone was confused about the party.

His phone buzzed again. It was a text from Adam Arlotta. He was super popular. Adam was the wrestling team's star.

"Not invited?" Adam wrote. "You mad at me, bro?"

He won Regionals... twice!

ADAM ARLOTTA

"OMG," Andrew said. "Adam thinks I'm mad at him."

More texts came in. People were shocked. They wanted to know why they were uninvited. Some thought the party was off. Others asked if they weren't cool enough. Most hoped it was a joke.

Andrew wanted to send another text. But he didn't know what to say.

"I've got to explain this," Andrew said. He was scared. His birthday might be ruined. Then he looked at Scott and Derek. "You guys will help me, right?"

"I don't know," Scott said slowly. "We *are* uninvited." He and Derek laughed.

"Sorry, Andrew," Derek said. "I'd love to help. But I've got a report to write."

"And I've got math," Scott said. "Hope you figure this out. Later!"

Andrew walked home alone. He was bummed. Texts kept coming in. Everyone was confused.

MidZone was buzzing too. Kids were making other plans. No one was coming to Andrew's party anymore.

"Andrew's party = OVER!" one post said.

"It's cool," another said. "No way it could beat last year's!"

Someone even made a meme. They used

Andrew's fifth grade yearbook photo. He had worn braces then. His hair stuck up all over. The words on it read, "I'm Andrew. You're not cool enough for my party."

Great. I'm a meme now.

Andrew Lu

Andrew wanted to fix this. There was one problem. He would have to explain everything. That meant admitting he had tried to trick Zach.

He would sound like a jerk. His parents would be mad too. They might cancel his party for real.

OMG, he thought. *This is the worst.*

5

JUST KIDDING?

Andrew lay on the couch. He didn't know what to do.

Texts kept coming. MidZone posts continued too. People bragged about not going to the party. They thought it was funny.

Andrew followed all the posts. He couldn't help it.

This can't be happening. Does everyone hate me? Am I not cool anymore?

Andrew's mom frowned at him. "Put down your phone."

"I can't," Andrew said. "It's for school. We have to watch something."

That was a lie. But he couldn't tell her the truth. Mrs. Lu and Zach's mom were friends. His mom couldn't find out. Andrew would be grounded. He would never have a party again.

His dad looked at him sternly. "It's time for dinner. You can watch it later. No phones at the table."

His mom smiled. "I'm proud of you, though. You're staying on top of your schoolwork."

Andrew smiled back. Inside, he felt guilty.
First he'd been a jerk to Zach. Now he was
lying to his parents.

He barely touched his dinner. Soon it was
time for bed.

I can't even eat Mom's yummy casserole.

Andrew couldn't take it anymore. He
pulled out his phone.

"Just kidding!" he texted. "My party is
still on. Gotcha!"

Andrew hit send. The text went to
everyone.

He copied the text. Then he posted it on
MidZone.

"That should do it," he said out loud.

Andrew went to bed. Within minutes, he was asleep.

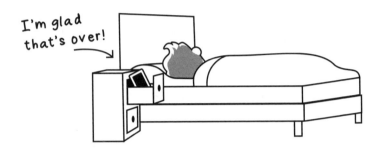

I'm glad that's over!

Buzz! Buzz!

Andrew woke up with a start. His phone was vibrating. *It's probably my friends,* he thought. *The party is still on.*

Andrew read the texts. His stomach dropped. He was wrong. All the texts were negative. Some people were angry. Others didn't believe him.

"Seriously?"

"Yeah, right."

"So uncool."

"Am I invited or not?"

"What a dumb joke."

"I don't even want to go now!"

"Sorry, bro. Made other plans."

MidZone was even worse. No one knew what to believe.

"What kind of joke is this?" Adam Arlotta wrote.

"This is stupid!"

"Way to ruin your own party!"

"This whole thing is a joke. And so is Andrew Lu."

"I'll be at the movies."

"No party for me!"

ANDREW'S PARTY
POPULATION: 0

Andrew groaned. His text hadn't been for everyone. He had meant it only for Zach Bottoms. Now everything was out of control.

More kids posted his old yearbook picture. His face was all over MidZone. One had "Party's Over!" on it. Another was just Andrew in a party hat. It was about him being alone on his birthday.

Party's Over!

Andrew's phone kept buzzing. He thought his head would explode.

"OMG!" he cried. "What now?"

Finally, he turned the phone off. Then he put it in a drawer.

6

NEXT LEVEL

The next day, Andrew got up late. His dad dropped him off at school. Immediately, things felt off.

As he walked in, everyone stared at him. He went to pull out his phone. It would give him something to look at. Then he wouldn't have to face others.

Oh no, Andrew thought. *Where is it?*

Wait, where's my phone?

Turning his phone off had been a relief. Andrew hadn't checked it all night. This morning, he was running late. He forgot to grab it before he left.

Oops...

"Dude. How are you even here?" Scott asked.

They were standing outside the gym. Everyone was heading to class. Many kids were still eyeing Andrew.

"And what's up with your phone?" Derek asked. "You didn't answer our texts."

"Yeah," Scott said. "We even tried calling you. It went to voice mail. I almost left one!"

He and Derek laughed. They thought

voice mail was old tech. The name even sounded funny.

"Why?" Andrew asked. "What's up?"

Before they could answer, Amanda Corona walked up. "Hey," she said to Andrew. "Are you okay?"

"Yeah. I'm fine."

"Cool," she replied. Then she walked away.

Andrew threw up his hands. "Okay. What's going on? Why is everybody looking at me?"

"They think you're sick," Scott said. "Like, almost-dead sick."

"Yeah," Derek said. "Rumors have been flying."

"What?" Andrew shrieked.

"There's more," Derek said. "Some people think you've been kidnapped."

"They think the kidnappers sent out that first text." Scott laughed. "Why else would you tell everyone they weren't invited?"

"And then re-invite them?" Derek laughed too.

Who would seriously believe that?!

Andrew glared at them. "What are you talking about? You both told me to send the texts!"

"We told you to send them to Zach," Scott said. "Then *you* uninvited everyone."

"Why didn't you help?" Andrew asked. "You could've talked to people."

Jayden Walters came over. He patted Andrew on the shoulder. "This is epic. Your party is the ultimate joke!"

Then he walked away.

"I told them the party was still on," Andrew said. "Why don't they believe me?"

"Well," Derek said. "It's probably all the pranks. No one knows when you're joking or not."

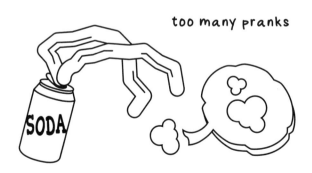

too many pranks

"Even we don't," Scott said.

Andrew sighed. "So nobody's coming to my party?"

"That's right," Derek said.

"OMG!" Andrew shouted.

Scott and Derek stared at him. They looked shocked.

More people looked at him now. Some were texting. A few took pictures. Others recorded videos.

Andrew turned. He sprinted to class. It was safer there.

7

MIDZONE EFFECT

It was Thursday morning. Andrew was walking to school. He didn't want to check MidZone. But he couldn't help it.

Don't even look!

7:43

Scott had texted him the night before. He'd told Andrew about more rumors. Now people thought the party was on. It just wasn't at Andrew's house.

Some thought it would be at Fun City. It

had rides and mini golf. Others said it was at Knight Meadows. That was a big concert hall. Ned's Groovy Ghosts were going to play. Andrew would sing with them.

A few said the party was in a secret location. No one knew where. Andrew would give out clues. It was going to be like a treasure hunt. The first 20 kids there would get prizes.

"This is nuts," Andrew had texted back. "People believe this? Why?"

After that, there was another rumor.

Now the party was at the local stadium. The baseball team was playing a special game. Andrew would pitch.

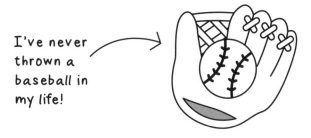

I've never thrown a baseball in my life!

He couldn't believe it. Everything was so messed up. *One text,* Andrew thought. *It caused all this.*

"Okay. What are you really planning?" Scott asked Andrew.

The boys were on their way to class. Scott walked on one side of Andrew. Derek was on the other. This was for protection. Students followed Andrew. All of them shouted questions.

"Where's the party?"

"Will a celebrity be there?"

"Can I bring my cousins?"

Andrew's stomach was in knots. He had wanted a cool party. But this was too much. He sighed. *Not even a huge waterslide is worth this.*

so much for the best party ever. . .

Closed!

Derek talked about the party too. "Let me guess. Is it better than all the rumors?"

The boys slid into an empty classroom. They shut the door. Kids were still yelling. Andrew couldn't take it anymore.

"OMG!" he said to Scott and Derek. "None

of that is happening. It's just a party. And it's at my house."

His friends stared at him.

Do they believe me? Andrew couldn't tell. "It'll still be great," he said. "Like always."

"Okay," Scott said slowly. "Nice try." He slapped Andrew on the back. "You almost had us!"

"Yeah." Derek smiled. "This is your best joke ever! We're your best friends. And even we don't know what's up. Make it epic!"

Just then, the bell rang. Scott and Derek headed for class.

"No!" Andrew called after them. "It's not—" But they just walked away.

Andrew waited until the hallway was empty. Then he made his way to first period.

A voice stopped him. "Hi, Andrew." It was Mr. Duncan. He taught history. "Happy birthday! I heard about your party. Knight Meadows? That's so cool. Ned's Groovy Ghosts rock."

Mr. Duncan owns every album Ned's Groovy Ghosts have made.

"Uh-huh," Andrew said. He hurried to class.

Wow, he thought. *Even teachers have*

heard the rumors. Why won't anyone listen to me? Have I played too many jokes?

A kid rushed past Andrew. It was Zach.

Andrew stared after him. Once, they had been friends. Zach had tried to explain. There hadn't been a lie. But Andrew wouldn't listen.

Just like no one is listening to me. Now he knew how it felt.

Andrew had been wrong. Then it hit him. He knew what he needed to do.

8

ONE LAST POST

Andrew had a plan. He thought about it all day.

After school, he went straight home. *No homework,* he thought. *Not even video games. I have to do this first.*

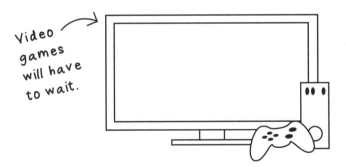

Video games will have to wait.

He pulled out his phone. Then he started to type on MidZone.

"Hi, everyone. There has been a lot of confusion about my party. This is my fault. I invited Zach Bottoms. Then I told him he wasn't invited. But I accidentally sent that text to everyone.

It was supposed to be a joke. But it wasn't funny. I see that now. And I'm sorry things got so mixed up.

I just want to be clear. None of the rumors are true. But my party is still happening. It's at my house. There will be food, music, and games. We'll have a waterslide too. But that's it.

You are all still invited. Zach, that includes you. I hope you come."

I mean it.

He took a deep breath. Then he posted it all.

The next day, everything seemed normal. Scott and Derek met up with Andrew. They told him they were coming to the party. Other kids did too.

Social media had quieted down. MidZone still had a few posts teasing Andrew. Some kids thought the prank wasn't done. Others were bummed. They wanted an epic party.

Most people were excited though. They knew Andrew's parties were fun.

Overall, Andrew felt better. Still, he hadn't heard from Zach.

"We shouldn't be having this party," Mrs. Lu huffed. Andrew and his parents were in the backyard. The party hadn't started yet.

A huge waterslide was being inflated. It was almost 40 feet tall. The slide dropped straight down. Then it went across the lawn. Finally, it fed into their pool. Andrew couldn't wait to test it.

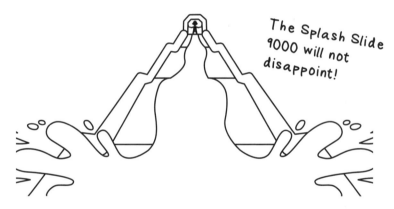

The Splash Slide 9000 will not disappoint!

Mr. Lu looked at his wife. "Honey, he messed up. But he tried to make it right."

Andrew had talked to his parents. He told them about his trick. They knew about the rumors too. His mom had been so mad. She had called Zach's mom.

"You were mean to Zach," Mrs. Lu said to Andrew. "He was your friend. His mom said he was so embarrassed."

"I'm sorry," Andrew said.

Mrs. Lu sighed. "I just don't know. A party? After all this? It doesn't feel right."

"It was wrong," Mr. Lu said. "And there will be consequences." He gave Andrew a stern look. "But the waterslide is already here. The food is too. We can't cancel now."

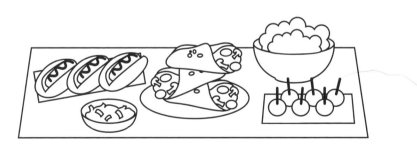

All this food would go to waste.

Mr. Lu looked at Andrew again. "I am glad you told the truth. Thank you for doing that."

Andrew nodded. Telling the truth had felt good. He was glad people had finally listened.

Zach had told Andrew the truth once too. But Andrew hadn't listened. *Will Zach listen to me now?* he wondered.

9

TALK IT OUT

OMG! Andrew thought. He was pumped. His party had started. People were arriving. Gifts were piling up. It was so awesome.

People showed up!

Scott and Derek were the first to get there. Andrew took them on the waterslide. He had already ridden it ten times.

Scott splashed into the pool. "That was amazing!" he yelled.

"I'm going again," Derek said. He got out of the pool. Then he ran back to the slide.

More kids arrived. Soon Andrew's backyard was crowded. People went in and out of the house. The party even spilled into the front yard.

Andrew's whole neighborhood was there. Kids ran around. They ate food. Some watched movies on the big screen. Others started a water balloon war. Everyone went on the slide. People were having a blast. Even Mr. and Mrs. Lu seemed more relaxed.

Andrew stood back. He watched all his friends having fun.

It had been a wild week. But everything had worked out. His party had turned out better than expected.

"Andrew," a voice called.

He turned and looked. It was Shannon Evers. She had just gotten out of the pool. A pink towel was wrapped around her waist.

Wow! Even Shannon came!

"Great party!" she said.

Andrew smiled. "Thanks."

"That slide is awesome. I can't believe how tall it is."

"Yeah," Andrew replied. "Me neither."

"Hey," Shannon continued. "I know this last week was weird. But it was cool of you to come clean. That must have been hard."

Andrew nodded. "It was the right thing to do."

It feels like a weight lifted.

"Shannon! Over here!" A group of girls waved.

"Well. I've got to go. Come say hi later, okay?"

"Sure."

"Happy birthday!"

Andrew felt good. His party was a hit. But he realized someone was missing.

It was Zach. Andrew wished he had come. He had apologized to Zach for the prank. But that was just in a post. Plus, he had never said sorry for dumping him in fifth grade.

I'd still be mad too.

That was still on Andrew's mind. It bothered him. Not having Zach there felt wrong.

I've got to fix this, Andrew thought. *But how?*

An idea sprang to his mind. His phone was charging in his room. Andrew went inside to get it. He just wanted to talk to Zach.

Andrew picked up his phone. He started to text Zach. Then he stopped.

Texting had begun this whole mess. Andrew called Zach instead.

He got his voice mail.

"Hey, Zach," Andrew said nervously. "Sorry about that messed-up text. I'm also sorry about ignoring you in fifth grade. You probably hate me. If you do, I totally understand. Either way, I miss you. And I want you to come to my party. We can play video games. Hope you can make it."

10

THE BEST GIFT

An hour went by. Everyone was still having a blast. The waterslide was a big hit. Kids lined up. They all wanted another ride. People played volleyball in the pool.

The food was great too. Andrew's parents were the best. They'd gotten Pizza Burritos to cater.

Andrew kept checking his phone. But there was nothing from Zach. He understood. Zach was probably mad. They might never be friends again. The thought made Andrew sad.

Suddenly, the waterslide made a loud noise. Andrew jumped. *What was that?*

"Hey!" a kid yelled from the top. "Where's the water?"

Hey! Where's the water?

Andrew looked. The water had stopped flowing. "Oh no," he said. "Is it broken?"

Mr. Lu went to check. There was a motor.

This pumped water onto the slide. It had been humming before. Now it was dead.

"Is it really broken, Dad?" Andrew asked.

Mr. Lu sighed. "Yes. I'm afraid so. And it's too late to call someone to fix it."

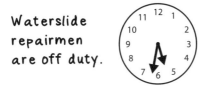

Waterslide repairmen are off duty.

All the kids groaned. The waterslide had been so fun. What would they do now?

Andrew started to get nervous. *Is the party over? Will people start leaving? What will they say on MidZone?*

"Hey," a voice called. "What's going on?"

Andrew turned. There was Zach. He was dressed in plaid swim trunks. A white towel was slung over his shoulder. His parents stood behind him.

Zach's dad was tall. He wore glasses just like Zach's. Mrs. Bottoms had short hair. She wore glasses too.

"Hey, Zach," Andrew said. He ran to greet him. "The slide just broke."

"It did?" Zach asked. "Let me see."

He walked over to the motor. His parents followed. They looked at it for a moment.

"Get me a screwdriver," Zach said. "I need a flathead."

"Bring a hammer too," Zach's dad said.

Mrs. Bottoms nodded. "We also need some oil."

"Okay," Mr. Lu said. He went to the garage.

"I'm glad you came," Andrew said to Zach.

"Me too." Zach smiled. "Thanks for calling. That meant a lot. I know how much you hate voice mail."

Andrew laughed. He wanted to say more. But he didn't have time. His dad was back with the tools.

We got this!

Zach and his parents went to work. They turned a few screws. Then they banged the hammer several times. Mrs. Bottoms applied some oil.

"Okay," Zach said. "Turn it back on."

"You fixed it?" Andrew asked him.

"I think so."

Andrew's dad flipped a switch. The motor hummed. Water started flowing.

"It's working!" Andrew cheered. "You did it!"

Everyone clapped. Zach took a bow. Then he laughed. Andrew did too.

People lined back up for the slide. The games continued. Andrew's party kept going strong. It was all thanks to Zach Bottoms.

"Hey," Andrew said to Zach. "Want to check out the slide? It's awesome."

"Sure."

They climbed the steps.

At the top, Andrew turned to Zach. "Listen. I'm really sorry for everything. Can you forgive me?"

Zach smiled. "It's okay. We're friends now, right?"

"Oh yeah!" Andrew fist-bumped Zach. "Forever."

"I'm glad," Zach said. "Now our first order of business is having fun!"

On second thought...

BEING COOL < HAVING FUN

"Alright!" Andrew shouted.

They counted to three. Then they both went down the slide. The boys zoomed across the lawn. Finally, they splashed into the pool.

"Wow!" Zach grinned. "That was amazing."

"Want to go again?" Andrew asked.

"I want to ride this slide a billion times!" Zach declared.

They climbed up again.

Andrew was excited. They still had the whole night. There was so much to do.

Soon there will be cake, he thought. *We can watch movies. And of course, there are presents.* Andrew looked at the huge pile. Then he looked at Zach.

I already got the best gift, he thought. *Zach is my friend again. Nothing can beat that.*

"OMG!" Andrew shouted at the top of the slide. "This is the best birthday ever!"